Mr. Turtle's Magic Glasses

JANE THAYER

pictures by
MAMORU
FUNAI

William Morrow and Company
New York

3177 7665

Princess Eliza lived in her father's castle,
and she was always busy at work or play.
She had to study books,
in order to talk wisely
with important people.
She studied French,
to murmur when the king of France came,
"Votre Majesté me fait un grand honneur,"
and Spanish, for saying to Spanish nobles,
"Buenas días, Don Carlos."

She learned fine needlework
and practiced piano scales.
And she worked arithmetic problems,
so that when the day came
for her to be queen
she could use the royal money
for the good of all.
When lessons were over,
Eliza leaped on her little black horse
and galloped along the castle trails,
or pedaled her bicycle swiftly
along the paths.
She bounced about the tennis court
and swam in the royal lake.

In fact, Princess Eliza was so used
to rushing around
that when she wasn't busy for five minutes
she was bored
and rushed to her mother, Queen Caroline,
complaining, "I haven't anything to do!
What can I do?"
Queen Caroline was a sweet woman,
who wandered about the castle
with her crown on crooked,
watering the flowers.
"Darling, must you always
be doing something?" she asked.
"Yes!" said Eliza, stamping her foot,
and rushed to find King Andrew, her father.
"I haven't anything to do! What can I do?"
King Andrew, who was sometimes bored himself
when he wasn't busy,
was anxious to see the Princess happy
so she wouldn't mind being queen someday.
"What would you like to do?" he asked.
"Go to a circus," suggested the Princess.
"Summon a circus,"
King Andrew commanded Lord Harold,
his head courtier.

A circus set up its tent on the castle lawn.
A trainer put trained bears through tricks.
A lady walked a tightrope
and swung on a high trapeze.
A clown shot out of a cannon.
Eliza clapped her hands.
Then she went back to her daily round
with a sigh.
"Would you care
to go to a carnival, my dear?"
the worried King asked.
Eliza rode on a Ferris wheel
and ate spun-sugar candy,
but this excitement too was soon over.

King Andrew took her to the horse races.
Eliza wore a new hat
and found the races exciting,
but when she went home to the castle
the King heard that sigh again.
Princess Eliza sighed more and more.
The minute she wasn't busy
she was bored, and sighed, and said,
"There's nothing to do
in this unexciting castle.
Maybe I'll run away."

King Andrew began to fear
that she might refuse to be queen,
and finally he decided to discuss the matter
with Queen Caroline.
He found her sitting in the garden,
her knitting idle in her lap.
"Our daughter is bored," he said.
"How can I keep her busy and happy
with day-to-day doings,
and willing to be the queen
when she grows up?"
He looked at his wife.
"You seem happy. What's your secret?"
"My darling husband, Your Majesty,"
said the Queen with a gentle smile,
"our child is like you.
She must always be doing something.
She wouldn't sit still long enough
for me to tell her my secret.

But perhaps,"
said Queen Caroline thoughtfully,
"a friend of mine could tell her."
"What friend?" said King Andrew.
"That friend," said Queen Caroline,
and pointed her knitting needle
at a turtle under a hollyhock leaf.
"That sounds pretty silly to me,"
said the King.
"Go away, dear," said the Queen.
"I must talk to Titus Turtle now."

So Titus T. Turtle was waiting
for the Princess next day.
But Eliza, racing by on her bicycle,
failed to see him in time.
Titus was turned upside down,
and only his shell saved him.

The Princess was a kind little girl,
and she jumped off her bicycle
to see if the turtle was hurt.
She turned him over.
Titus stuck out his head and said,
"I wish to talk to Your Royal Highness."

"Oh, good!" said Princess Eliza,
and sat down on a small garden throne
that happened to be there.
"Your Royal Highness," said Titus severely,
"you have no respect for humble creatures."
"Why, yes I have," said the Princess.
"I didn't see you, that's all."
"You don't see *anything*," said Titus.
"I wish to make you a present
of some magic glasses."
"How exciting! What shall I see?" cried Eliza.
"Beautiful, interesting things.
Humble creatures. Even a few miracles.
But this will require cooperation."
"I'll cooperate," she promised.
"Put them on," said Titus,
handing her the glasses.
Eliza put them on.
"I don't see anything different."
"Sit still and look," ordered Titus.
Eliza was not used to sitting still
and she found doing so quite difficult.
She wiggled and the glasses fell off.
"You said you'd cooperate.
Sit still!" commanded Titus.

After a while she sat still.
The glasses stayed firmly on her royal nose,
and suddenly as she looked about she cried,
"See that beautiful spider web
spun from flower to flower.
It gleams like gold in the sun!"
"What else?" said Titus.

"The dewdrops on that round green leaf
flash just like diamonds!"
"Good. Come back tomorrow,
Your Highness," said Titus.
"But give me the glasses.
You'd never keep them on your nose
the way you rush around,
and besides you must wear them
only when your duties are done."
"You said I'd see some miracles,"
the Princess reminded him.
"All in good time," he told her.

Bored with her everyday life
and eager to see a miracle,
Princess Eliza came back.
Little by little she learned to sit still,
keeping the glasses on her nose.
Of course, she had seen birds before,
but never had she watched
an oriole feed its young.
Or a hummingbird sip from the lilies,
then rest in a lilac bush.
Or chickadees wait in line for the birdbath.

She had seen ants and butterflies and toads,
but never had she watched
ants build an ant highway,
a butterfly hunt the right leaf
on which to lay her eggs,
a toad burst out of his skin and eat it up.

She sat wide-eyed as a shrew
stole out and squealed at a squirrel.
She smiled when a baby field mouse
played with its tail
and a little rabbit leaped about
to scare a blue jay away.
"I never knew," she whispered,
"so much was going on!"
"You never had magic glasses,"
Titus pointed out.

"And now that you can keep them
on your royal nose
we shall arrange a miracle."
He held out a little hard seed.
"Plant this by the garden wall, water it,
and watch through your magic glasses."
She jumped up in excitement,
and her glasses fell off.
"You will never keep the glasses on your nose,
which means you'll never see a miracle,
unless you slow down.
And sit *still*," said Titus crossly.
"I'll remember," said Eliza meekly.
"But how does a turtle know about
beautiful, interesting things?"
"Turtles don't rush around," he informed her,
and now the Princess saw
that he wore magic glasses too.
Her lady-in-waiting, Eleanor,
carried the little hard seed
on a crystal plate.
Princess Eliza took her time
and kept the glasses on.
Titus carried his shell
to the shade of a hollyhock leaf.

Then Lord Harold, the head courtier,
brought out the royal tools and dug a hole.
Eliza dropped in the seed.
The Lady Eleanor dragged out the royal hose.
Eliza watered.

The Princess sat on a small garden throne
and watched,
keeping the magic glasses on her royal nose.
She hardly knew that
the Queen came quietly to sit beside her.
She saw tiny green leaves
spring from the little hard seed.
She saw a vine begin to twine
against the garden wall.

And one morning soon after sunrise
a morning glory, bluer than the blue sky,
opened wide.
"It *is* a miracle!" whispered Eliza,
who had watched through her magic glasses
a little hard seed turn into a lovely flower.
"Yes, darling," said Queen Caroline.
"What's this about a miracle?"
said King Andrew, coming out.

"You have to have magic glasses to see one,"
his daughter said.
Then she cried,
"Mother, you've got magic glasses too!
Have you always had them?"
"Yes, darling," said the Queen.
"Shall we get your father a pair,
if he can sit still?"

"Here, Your Majesty.
Extra strong," said Titus.
Then each day when their duties were done,
King Andrew, Queen Caroline,
and Princess Eliza sat in the garden,
or wandered among
the flowers, the pools, and the woods,
keeping the magic glasses on their noses.

Eliza saw things she had never noticed,
including quite a few miracles.
She watched a duckling break out of an egg.
Tadpoles turn into frogs.
A spider spin a gossamer pouch for her eggs.
An ugly green worm in a silken cocoon
hatch into a butterfly.

"Oh, Father," she exclaimed,
"even when I'm the queen
I can put on my magic glasses!
I can see exciting things—
even miracles—any day!"
Under his hollyhock leaf, Titus mumbled,
"You'll be a better queen too.
Respect for humble creatures."
"And Father," said the Princess,
"it's pretty miraculous
that a turtle can talk.
I never knew that, did you?"
"I did not," said the King.
"But it seems your mother knew."
"Yes, dears," said Queen Caroline.